dreamlike
states

BRIAN JAMES FREEMAN

CEMETERY DANCE PUBLICATIONS

Baltimore
❖ 2013 ❖

Cemetery Dance Publications
132-B Industry Lane, Unit #7
Forest Hill, MD 21050
http://www.cemeterydance.com

First Limited Edition Printing

ISBN-13: 978-1-58767-332-0
ISBN-10:   1-58767-332-0

Cover Artwork Copyright © 2013 by Vincent Chong
Interior Artwork Copyright © 2013 by Glenn Chadbourne
Interior Design by Kate Freeman Design

For Serenity Richards

With special thanks to Kathryn for helping me get through these once and for all; to Norman Prentiss, Robert Brouhard, and Brad Saenz for the technical support; to Ed Gorman for the humbling introduction; to Vincent Chong and Glenn Chadbourne for the pitch-perfect artwork; and to Richard Chizmar, Nanci Kalanta, and Elizabeth and Tom Monteleone for giving these stories a home in the first place.

table of contents

introduction

BY ED GORMAN

as someone who edited *Mystery Scene* magazine, I witnessed the disappearance of many promising writers. I don't say this with any pleasure of course; stillborn careers are sad. I think it's exciting to read somebody new you can start recommending to everybody who'll listen.

Some of the young writers I pushed in the magazine went on to become prominent names in mystery and dark suspense. A handful of them became genre bestsellers. One or two hit the *New York Times* Best Seller List. This wasn't because of our magazine. It was because many other writers, reviewers and editors were just as excited about them as I was. And it worked both ways. Whenever I'd read a review that extolled the pleasures of a fresh new voice, I'd buy the book immediately and give it a read. I wanted to be impressed and many times was. And I'd then talk it up.

But then there were the disappeared. Each of them had a different story. Some got sick, some got bad into drugs or drink, some had personal tragedies and some seemed to say everything in one or two books. And a few died.

Every once in awhile when I'm in Half-Price Books, I see the spines of very good books that take me back ten, twenty years and I wonder where the hell he or she is now and what he or she is doing. A few years ago I had lunch with one of the disappeared, a man who'd written three excellent novels and then quit. He explained his absence this way: "After I found out about all the bullshit that goes with working with publishers,

I just quit. The bullshit just killed my desire to write any more."

Pardon, if you will, this rather long introduction to my introduction of Brian James Freeman. See, Brian started publishing in high school and has grown in skill and stature with every story and novella and novel. His book *The Painted Darkness* pleased the likes not only of reviewers and readers but also of other writers such as Tess Gerritsen, Stewart O'Nan, David Morrell, Bentley Little and Richard Matheson. Raymond Chandler once described *The Great Gatsby* as "a little pure art." I thought of Chandler's phrase as I read Brian's book.

In other words, Brian has been building his career carefully, starting out in high school and getting so consistently better that the writers mentioned above—and those are just a handful of the writers who've praised him—are happy to tell the world just how good he is. He will not become one of the disappeared. Of that I'm certain.

He has the talent, the fire, and he produces at his own pace. Smart.

There's another reason I'm sure he'll not only be around but will become a major voice in serious fiction. His artistry.

To quote my friend Brian Keene, "Brian James Freeman is not merely a craftsman, he is an artisan...His stories are entertaining...but they transcend that as well."

If you've had the pleasure of reading Freeman's *Black Fire* or *Blue November Storms* or any of the stories collected here, you already appreciate the truth of Brian Keene's words.

Brian James Freeman had the magic from the start. Yes, he gets better, but he can sit down and read all his old stories with pride. Many of my writer friends smile when the conversation turns to their early stories and novels. One of my buddies calls his first two novels "wincers," meaning that there are word choices, plot choices and leaden attempts at characterizations that make him wince when he reads them now. I go right past wincing; I go all the way to nausea. There are early stories of mine I won't re-read. I have a sense of how bad they are and if I were to scan them again I know they'd be even worse than I remembered.

But now to the stories in the book you're about to read. Here are a few of the thoughts I wrote down as I read them.

Isolation is the constant theme. Physical and mental isolation. The hardy pulp theme of one man triumphing over great odds works for most writers but doesn't seem to appeal to Brian.

I don't know how much Cornell Woolrich Brian has read. Maybe none at all. But in the majority of these stories we are presented with two of Woolrich's favorite set-ups: a phantasmagoric opening situation and a continuing, merciless sense of dislocation and dread. Action heroes need not apply. *Dreamlike States*, the title of this collection, says it best.

"One Way Flight," one of my favorites here, is claustrophobic in every respect. Not only does the protagonist face a phantasmagoric situation, he must try to confront it while trying to make sense of the impossible. Brian depicts the kind of panic that is really a form of insanity. When the character discovers what's really going on he is more isolated than ever. True facts: "One Way Flight" gave me nightmares three nights running.

In the masterful stories "A Dreamlike State" and "The Silent Attic," Brian produces melancholy and chilling tales that touch on the form known as The Unreliable Narrator. The hallucinatory aspects of the story enhance the delirium at the center of the pieces. What would merely be a device in other hands—madness of the protagonist—here brings depth and complexity to character.

But for all the skill and artistry, Brian's work never cheats the reader looking for pure entertainment.

As I read "The Gorman Gig" and "The Silent Attic," I imagined them as half hour TV episodes. Knock-out episodes. And of course, think of "One

Way Flight" filmed as a half hour TV episode—if done right, unforgettable horror.

So let's face it: I am an enthusiastic admirer of Brian James Freeman's work and don't hesitate to tell everyone I can. If you've read him already, you know what I'm talking about. If you haven't, it's time to turn the page and become acquainted with his work. I think you'll find yourself tracking down his other books as soon as you turn the last page of this one.

as she lay there dying

the roads were wet from another morning of April showers, and the co-ed freshman lying on the pavement was missing part of her head. Her legs were twisted awkwardly under her body and there was blood on the sidewalk. One of her tattered running shoes had landed on the other side of the street, knocked clear of the scene of the accident. A broken iPod lay just beyond her hand.

The dying girl wore mesh shorts and a pink shirt featuring the Haverton Field Hockey logo. She was sprawled next to the curb at the entrance to the school's grounds, directly in front of the big stone wall with the sign proclaiming "Welcome to Haverton College." The car that had hit her was nowhere to be seen.

"Oh shit," Sam whispered, turning to the bushes and vomiting. The English professor wasn't alone in his horror.

A secretary named Marge Wilson held the girl's hand. At the time of the accident Marge had been walking to the pizza parlor just off campus to pick-up lunch for her co-workers, and a wad of cash was still in her left hand, forgotten. She had seen everything.

Students on their way to one o'clock classes gathered around the dying girl. Some held their hands to their faces while others texted their friends.

The dying girl moaned. Her disfigured head rolled loosely on her rubbery neck and blood spit from her broken mouth. Her teeth were red.

She turned her face blindly toward Sam and she whispered in clipped breaths: "Sammy, we can't run anymore."

Sam blinked, startled by the sound of his name. He stared into the girl's glassy eyes. He didn't recognize her, but no one called him Sammy, especially not students. The only person who ever called him that had been dead for six months.

Then Sam heard the artificial click and whirl as a camera phone snapped a photo.

"Get out of here, you ass," Sam said, turning and shoving the young man with a backpack slung over his shoulder. The student stumbled backwards and then just stood there, off balance and stunned. Sam yelled and shoved him again, right up against the stone wall with the school's name.

Next came more shouting, but the rest was a blur as the campus police arrived and then the ambulance—the girl was dead by then—and the questioning began.

———

According to one of the department secretaries gossiping in the third floor hallway of McGrove Hall, the dead girl's name was Lauren Redman, a first year Math Ed major from the other side of the state who came to the school on a field hockey scholarship.

Sam listened as he posted a note on his office door, canceling his classes for the rest of the week. He couldn't stand the idea of facing the slack jawed students while their obvious boredom burned a hole right through him.

Not today.

———

Walking home to his cozy neighborhood outside the small college town, Sam took a side street to avoid the main entrance to the school. The girl's blood would still be there.

What am I going to do? Sam thought, not for the first time.

As far as he could remember, the dead girl hadn't taken his mandatory Intro course, but the thousands of names and faces had blurred together over the years, so he couldn't be sure.

Actually, everything was a little blurry these days. Sam's shoving match with the cell phone voyeur felt like a distant memory of something he only witnessed. He didn't know what had come over him, but maybe it was a knee-jerk reaction to someone disrespecting the dying.

If that student had been there and photographed Julie when she died, Sam probably wouldn't have stopped with a shove. But his wife had died alone, with no one to hold her hand and comfort her. Sam hadn't even known she was dead until an hour later.

Did Lauren Redman really say, *Sammy, we can't run anymore,* as she lay there dying on the pavement?

Those words disturbed Sam, but he didn't know why. The poor girl was dead. Why was he so bothered by her last words? She probably had a boyfriend named Sammy. Or a brother. It was a common name. Just because *he* was standing there didn't mean she was speaking to him. She probably had no idea where she was, let alone that she was dying.

The words didn't mean *anything*. They were just a result of the last firing synapses as what remained of her brain shutdown. Some fragment of a memory.

This conclusion should have comforted Sam, but it didn't. He just kept hearing the words over and over in the dead girl's halting voice:

Sammy, we can't run anymore.

———

Sam entered the foyer of the house he had shared with his wife until her sudden death and he stopped in the doorway.

Like always, he vividly recalled every detail of the day he arrived home from a run and discovered he was a widower.

He closed his eyes and relived it again for the hundredth time.

And why not? What else was he going to do tonight?

———————

On the morning Julie died, Sam was soaked from head to toe in sweat, his feet ached, and his legs moved like they were made of marble as he paced the driveway to cool down and keep his muscles from tightening up. The winter air clung to his exposed flesh and steam rose from his clothes. Two hours of running had never felt better than it did in these moments when the pain and the joy were still fresh.

If there was anything wrong inside the house, he didn't know it yet. His mind was just starting to come down from his runner's high, the rush of endorphins that washed away all of the pains, distractions, and annoyances of the real world.

No matter how badly his legs hurt when he finished a run, his mind was always clear and ready to face new challenges. Julie had taught him this trick not long after they first met on a blind date. She called running her secret weapon for a long and happy life.

This particular morning, though, after Sam completed his cool-down routine, he tried to open the front door and found something had been pushed up against it from the inside.

He had to shove the door open to discover Julie lying at the bottom of the steps, a tiny pool of blood next to her head. Her iPod was still clutched in her hand like a talisman and her arms were twisted under her body, as if she had fallen down the steps.

She was dressed in her purple jogging suit with her top still zipped. That meant she hadn't made it out the door for *her* morning run, which usually started an hour after Sam's most Sundays. She ran for speed, her husband ran for distance.

dreamlike states

Sam stared at his wife's motionless body, then he knelt and very gently touched her wrist.

———————

"You love your melodramatic English Department bullcrap," Julie said to Sam one evening early in their marriage while she helped him out of his suit at the end of a long day. This was a few months after they moved into the house and nothing was really unpacked yet.

Sam had just finished telling her about the latest crisis in his department. Was that the time the janitorial service cut back to only emptying the office trashcans every other day? It was hard to keep all of the crap straight, year after year, and he still couldn't believe how much bitching and moaning his well-paid colleagues with seventeen-hour work weeks could muster about such trivial matters and perceived slights.

"What do you mean?" he asked.

"If everyone in your department wasn't a little insane, you'd be bored to tears and you know it," Julie said, slipping her fingers into the elastic band around his waist.

Sam couldn't deny the truth in her statement, especially considering his underwear came off before he could reply and they spent the rest of the evening in the bedroom.

That was one of the many good times they had shared in their ten years of marriage, and there were so many good times he couldn't even count them, but he didn't think it was fair those moments were done and gone forever.

Their ten years of marriage had been wonderful, but he had been promised a lifetime.

————

Upon finding his wife's dead body and touching her cool wrist, Sam whispered, "This isn't melodramatic English Department bullcrap" for reasons he still didn't understand.

Julie might have been able to explain it to him. She saw things differently than he did, after all, and that was what made them perfect for each other.

Then, with his hand still on Julie's wrist, Sam asked the quiet house: "What am I going to do?"

———————

Every time Sam opened the front door of his home, he expected Julie to be there, dead again, but she never was, of course.

Julie was buried in the Haverton Community Cemetery on the far side of town, and Sam walked to her grave three or four times a week during his lunch break to discuss the latest news and drama with her, just like the old days.

Today Sam had wanted Julie's input on his big decision: whether to take a year's sabbatical and use it to pursue some other career.

Like always, he had sat on the ground and ate the peanut butter and jelly sandwich he brought from home, leaning against her granite marker and picking at the grass around the base, keeping everything neat and tidy. The day was overcast and forlorn. Sometimes he felt like the funeral had never ended.

To his credit, Sam never actually heard Julie reply to any of his questions or observations, but he liked the idea that maybe she was out there somewhere, listening. He didn't really buy into the whole afterlife concept, but if it were possible for Julie to still somehow exist on some other level of the universe, Sam would gladly change his beliefs in a heartbeat.

She probably would have the answers he needed, too. What to do with the rest of his life was a pressing decision for Sam. He had to request the sabbatical by Friday if the paperwork was to be approved in time for the fall schedule.

Sam understood he wasn't doing the students any good right now. He had cancelled more classes than he had attended this semester. At any other job he would have been fired, but he had tenure and the union wouldn't let anything happen to his position, of course.

Sam's livelihood wasn't in any danger. He could just put himself on cruise control and retire with full benefits at the age of sixty. Plenty of his colleagues were already on the thirty-and-out plan, after all. It was practically tradition.

But what would he do with all of the years to follow? Would he sit around the house writing reams of so-so poetry and watching television? Would he go to his desk and read old syllabi and pretend he missed his glory days? What kind of life would that be?

Besides, putzing along at work for a couple of decades without giving a crap wasn't the way Sam wanted to live. He wanted to really be *alive*.

Of course, he also wanted Julie by his side to carry out their plans—the fixer-upper in the country, the beach house, the second honeymoon to Bermuda, the babies, all the beautiful babies—but that was the most impossible dream he still clung to with a quiet desperation.

No one seemed to be holding Sam's inattentiveness at work against him, at least. Most people understood the grief of the unexpected death of the person who made your life feel so complete and full of purpose.

Who could blame Sam for not wanting to discuss Colonial Period American Literature while he was still attempting to comprehend how his beautiful bride, who was in better shape than him, could have been felled by an aneurysm while coming down the steps for her morning run, her brain shutting off before she even landed on the cold linoleum floor?

As far as Sam could tell, no one cared that his classes were falling so far behind, least of all the students.

———

Standing there in the foyer again, Sam wondered if the parents of Lauren Redman had been notified yet.

They were probably driving across the state right now to visit her in the morgue, to confirm her identity.

Sam believed the only thing worse than finding your beloved dead on the foyer floor was getting that dreaded phone call and making that drive, half your heart wanting to believe it would just turn out to be a terrible misunderstanding.

With Julie, Sam knew his wife was dead the moment he found her. There was no mistaken identity. There was no hoping for a miracle.

He guessed he should be grateful for that, but he wasn't. Julie was still dead, either way.

———

After Julie's death, Sam developed a condition that reminded him of a phenomenon he heard about all the time in his field. The symptoms snuck up on him from out of nowhere and he was deep in the affliction before he realized what was happening. He blamed the grief.

Truman Capote, Ralph Ellison, Harper Lee, Samuel Taylor Coleridge, Arundhati Roy, Gabriel Garcia Márquez, and Arthur Rimbaud all knew variations of the condition quite well, even if some of them suffered from it before the phrase was officially coined: writer's block.

Only Sam's problem wasn't with his writing. He continued to churn out poetry at his normal rate and he had updated his notes and syllabi for next semester without issue, just in case he felt a renewed vigor for teaching or simply couldn't pull the trigger on the sabbatical.

Sam didn't have *writer's* block. He had *runner's* block.

The last time he even tried to run—maybe a month after Julie's death when he desperately needed to escape from the world—was so dreadful that he held no ambition to make another attempt, not if he lived to be a hundred years old.

Like most people with a block, Sam understood what he wanted to do, but his mind wouldn't
let him, which created a little cycle of hell for him
to experience again and again. He needed to run
so badly some days, but even the thought of wear-
ing his running clothes could push him to tears.

The last time Sam had tried to go for a run,
he sat on the edge of the bed and tied his running
shoes, convinced this time would be different. He
loved running. The act of getting out there and at-
tacking the road was the only thing he had left in
life that could truly make him feel good—and this
time everything would be okay, he just knew it.

Sam stood, stretched, and then headed down
the stairs, his mind clear and his heart full of con-
fidence, but he never even made it outside.

When he reached the last step, he tripped and
fell, landing hard on the linoleum floor, sending a
dull ache through his bones. He found himself in
a position strikingly similar to Julie's death pose,
and he cried for over an hour, his entire body
shaking uncontrollably.

He hadn't put on those shoes since.

———————

Sam had never realized grief could run so deep and be so all consuming, but these days he truly understood the misery of knowing you'd never be able to have the one thing you needed most to fill a gaping emptiness in your world.

The love of his life was gone, he couldn't run, and he didn't want to teach anymore...so what was the point of riding the Earth around the sun year after year after year?

That was the question his mind would get stuck on in his darkest hours. He knew there was an easy answer to that question, and the ease with which he sometimes contemplated that answer scared him badly.

As darkness settled across the land, ending yet another lonely day, Sam couldn't help but think of Lauren Redman's final words again: *Sammy, we can't run anymore.*

A few hours later, Sam was dreaming, and in this dream he was running, following the trail around campus.

His legs had never felt better and there was no pain. He could go a hundred miles if he wanted. Maybe more.

Sam was calm and collected as the campus rolled past him like a groovy Technicolor background. The sun was shining brightly through the trees and everything was incredibly vivid and alive. Birds were singing. A breeze cooled his sweaty skin.

Sam couldn't remember spring ever being this beautiful and he never wanted this run to end, but as he neared a small wooden bridge over a stream, he saw two women jogging in his direction.

This wasn't unusual considering how many students frequented the trail, except for one important detail: both of these women were dead.

They were running side by side and they were smiling, showing off their bloody teeth. Julie's hair was maroon from the small pool of blood she had died in. The top of Lauren's head was missing and bits of gray matter were speckled across her pink field hockey shirt.

Sam tripped and stumbled to his knees as all of the color drained from the dream.

Then he screamed.

The two dead women looked at him, startled, and screamed back.

Their mouths were open so wide.

Their teeth were caked in dirt and blood... and then they shielded their faces with bruised and broken fingers.

They had clawed their way out of their graves.

———

Sam fell out of bed, soaked in sweat, his heart racing.

He crawled across the bedroom floor and into the master bathroom, where he lay in the dark and sobbed.

Until now he hadn't experienced a single bad dream after Julie's death, but this one was like a thunderbolt through his head.

Sleep was the one place he could escape after each long, painful day, but now his peaceful slumber had been stolen from him.

He was cold and lonelier than he had ever felt in his entire life. He really wasn't prone to melodrama like some of the prima donnas in his department, but he was completely overwhelmed and exhausted and disoriented by the nightmare. Every moving shadow made him cringe in terror.

This was all too much.

What was he going to do?

He couldn't live with nightmares like that.

He simply couldn't.

He couldn't run, he couldn't sleep, and his wife was dead.

What am I going to do, Sam thought. *What am I going to do?*

What could he possibly do?

Sam closed his eyes and sobbed, and he hated the answer that came to mind again and again and again.

———————

A few hours later, Sam opened his eyes.

Sunlight had slipped between the curtains and into his bedroom, washing over him where he lay on the cold bathroom tiles.

Next to him were the running shoes he had given up when he realized his days of pounding the pavement were probably over.

He had no memory of retrieving them from the closet where he had tossed them with a mixture of sadness and disgust.

Sam looked at the shoes, caked in dirt and grass stains.

He heard the dying student whisper: *Sammy, we can't run anymore.*

Sam didn't believe in messages from beyond the grave, yet those dying words were true for both Julie and Lauren, weren't they?

Neither of them could run anymore...but Sam could still run. What the hell was runner's block anyway? He hadn't run in almost six months and why? Because his mind was somehow stopping him?

"What a load of melodramatic bullcrap," Sam whispered.

He put on his running shorts, a gray t-shirt with the Havertown College logo, and his running socks with the extra padding on the heals.

Finally, Sam laced up the shoes. They felt just right.

He took the stairs slowly, his hand on the railing the entire way, careful to avoid a repeat of what happened the last time he tried to run.

When he reached the foyer, Sam opened the front door without stopping to second-guess his decision.

A few minutes later, he was jogging toward town and he didn't look back, not even once.

———

Sam understood where he was headed as soon as he made it out the front door: the trail around campus.

He passed by the entrance to the school where Lauren Redman died in a puddle of blood, probably not even aware that her run had come to a tragic end.

He locked his eyes on the road ahead of him and he ran even harder.

When Sam reached the start of the trail, his heart was pounding, but he couldn't slow down, not yet.

His legs were thundering under him like he was charging into battle.

Sam certainly wasn't expecting to see Julie and Lauren crossing the bridge in the woods, but he had to run across the bridge for himself.

They wouldn't be there. He knew that. He was certain of that. It simply wasn't possible for a million different reasons.

And when Sam reached the bridge, the dead women were nowhere to be seen…but for a man who didn't expect to see anyone, Sam was maybe a little too relieved.

————

Ten minutes later, Sam arrived at the bottom of the hill in the Haverton Community Cemetery. His clothing was soaked in sweat, his heart was pounding like a jackhammer, his lungs were tight, and he hadn't felt this good in a long time. It was as if an enormous weight had been lifted from his shoulders.

The sun was blazing brightly above the mountains to the east and the world was more beautiful than Sam ever remembered it being, even in the early days of his marriage when *everything* was picturesque and perfect. Every blade of grass shimmered in the sunlight. Every birdcall was a love song.

Sam had never felt relief like this. The darkness smothering him had been stronger and deeper than he ever realized.

This experience was more than his usual runner's high that lifted him away from the pains and displeasures of the real world. This was the cure to end all cures.

Julie had been right, as she always was. Running really was the secret to a long and happy life.

Today Sam wasn't running from despair and loneliness, he was running toward a bright and welcoming future.

But as he reached the hill where Julie was buried, Sam slowed to take in his surroundings. There was a change in the air. His vision and his senses were still clouded from the runner's high, but when he really concentrated, he could hear shoes pounding the pavement behind him.

He stopped, frozen by the sound. Those shoes were the only thing he could hear and they were suddenly so loud. No wind, no rustling of grasses, no birds in the sky. Other than those shoes, he was deaf.

The land grew dark again and Sam couldn't force himself to look back and see who might be coming. His newfound colorful world was being drained of light and life and he was terrified.

There were now heavy, rapid-fire breaths behind Sam as the person got closer and closer. The impacts of the shoes echoed around Sam as if he was locked inside some kind of vault.

Inside his ears, a voice whispered: *Sammy, we can't run anymore.*

Sam stumbled forward in the direction of Julie's grave.

There was someone standing at the top of the hill.

The person was merely a silhouette against the gray sun. She raised her arms, reaching out toward Sam.

He ran and the world grew bright again, full of colors and sounds that were wonderful and overwhelming.

Sam basked in the light and all of his pain melted away, returning him to that comfortable place, the place he never wanted to leave again.

He understood he had to keep running if he wanted this beautiful day to continue. He dug deep inside himself and ran even harder, the dark figure growing ever closer.

Sam prepared to embrace whatever he found at the top of the hill.

CHADBOURNE

one way flight

When he awoke, the man in seat 36-B had three very clear and terrifying thoughts go through his mind all at the same time.

The first thought: he had no idea who he was or how he got on the plane.

The second thought: all of the other passengers were either dead or asleep…and considering it was a bright sunny day outside, he had a pretty good idea they wouldn't be waking up anytime soon.

The third thought: 82726782B might be faulty.

That last thought didn't make a lot of sense, but considering he had no idea who he was or how he got onto a plane full of dead people, that seemed to be the least of his problems.

Panic gripped the passenger and his stomach turned at the mere thought of what he needed to do to confirm his situation, but he did it fast before he lost his nerve. He touched the face of the overweight man next to the window–not breathing, flesh cold–and then he touched the baby lying on the seat between him and the aisle–tiny eyes open and staring at him like cold, dark pebbles, but also dead. No sign of visible trauma or blood on either of them.

The passenger turned away from the baby's accusing stare and he searched the compartment again for any sign of life. There was no movement. He heard nothing other than the hum of the engines and the hiss of air coming through the vents. The plane was full of dead people. He still couldn't quite wrap his brain around the idea.

He didn't have a clue who he was and *all the other passengers were dead.*

Passenger 36-B shook his head, trying his best to clear his thoughts. How did this happen? Was he the only person left alive? What would he do if that was the case? Did he know the overweight man? What about the baby? He didn't remember having a kid…but then again, he didn't remember very much at the moment. He didn't feel any sort of recognition when he looked at the tiny child, only fear and pity.

Passenger 36-B unbuckled his seatbelt, stood, and inched out into the aisle, moving carefully so his hand wouldn't come close to the dead baby again.

Everyone was dead.

His heart jumped at the thought, as if some true understanding of his predicament was finally setting in. He was in a world of trouble.

"How could this have happened?" he asked. He didn't expect an answer, but it felt good to speak aloud, even if he didn't recognize his own voice. Hearing the words made him feel alive among all the dead. It reminded him that he *was* still alive, and if he wanted to stay that way, he needed to find some answers fast. So he asked himself again: *how could this have happened?*

The most obvious conclusion was terrorism. Nerve gas pumped in through the air system? It might explain all the dead passengers and maybe why he, apparently the lone survivor, was suffering from amnesia. Not that he knew anything about nerve agents. Or anything about anything for that matter. Right now he was simply happy to be alive and aware of his surroundings–bizarre and terrifying as they were.

Passenger 36-B checked his pockets for a wallet or some form of identification. At least then he would know his name, and maybe that knowledge would jog his memory of how he got on the plane and where he was headed and maybe what had happened. He searched the right pocket and then the left and then his back pockets, but they were all empty. Not even a stick of gum.

Where was I traveling without any identification? How'd I get on the plane? he wondered as he double-checked his pockets again, just to make sure he hadn't missed something. There was nothing to be found. A thought entered his mind, although he had no idea what it meant: *This was a one way flight.*

"One way flight?" he repeated. Again his voice sounded strange and alien to him. "What the hell does that mean?"

Even though he had no credit card, Passenger 36-B reached for the nearest air-phone. He figured it couldn't hurt to try. There was no dial tone. Was that normal? He wasn't sure, so he dialed a variety of numbers, including good old Zero for the Operator, but the phone didn't connect him to anyone. He dropped it with a sensation of regret, as if his best chance for answers had somehow slipped away.

But should he have been so surprised? If someone had been able to slip something into the air system to kill everyone onboard, surely they could have disabled the phones, right?

The plane shook a little as it hit a pocket of turbulence. A second later Passenger 36-B heard a thud at the rear of the plane.

"Hello?" he called out, moving in the direction of the sound.

There was a restroom after the last seat. The little panel in the door was green and said VACANT, but Passenger 36-B opened the door anyway. Maybe someone was hiding inside and hadn't locked the door.

There *was* someone inside, a tall man leaning against the small sink, his arms folded, his head turned and pushed against the wall. Like the others, he was dead and there was no blood and no sign of any visible wounds.

Passenger 36-B closed the door and surveyed the section again. He leaned over to a small window and peered outside.

It was a beautiful day, barely a cloud in the sky. Field after field passed by below, but there was nothing to identify where they were flying to or from…not that landmarks would necessarily tell him anything given the state of his memory.

The plane began a slow bank to the right, and Passenger 36-B put his hand against the overhead compartment to brace himself. That was when the most important question of all popped into his head: *who is flying the plane?*

He hurried to the front of the section, pushed aside the curtain, and stepped into the plush luxury of First Class. There were more dead passengers here, sitting on bigger seats with better legroom for their useless legs.

A flight attendant was slumped against a beverage cart in the middle of the aisle, as if whatever happened had overtaken everyone so quickly she didn't even have time to sit.

Passenger 36-B slipped past her as the plane banked downward sharply. He reached out to grab a seat to brace himself, but the plane hit another pocket of turbulence and tossed him to the side and his hands clutched a cold, lifeless head instead.

He quickly let go and fell to the floor, barely stopping the scream in his throat. He wasn't sure why he had bothered to control his terror. He could yell as loud as he wanted to, for as long as he wanted to, and he wouldn't wake anyone up.

Maybe there's someone onboard who shouldn't hear you coming.

The thought popped into his mind from out of nowhere, speaking in a voice he had never heard before (as far as he could remember), and although he had no idea where the words came from, he had to agree with the logic. For now, staying as quiet as possible might be a really good idea.

The plane continued to descend.

Passenger 36-B climbed to his feet again and returned his attention to the cockpit door, which was closed. He approached it slowly, listening for any sounds that could indicate who was inside. After all, maybe *that* was where the terrorists had gone. They could be flying the plane!

If there were three or four terrorists in there, he'd be outnumbered. Then again, he would have the advantage of taking them by surprise, however limited such an advantage might be. Was he willing to sacrifice himself if terrorists really were in control of the cockpit?

He didn't think he had much of a choice. If they had killed all of the passengers and crew, they wouldn't hesitate to kill him if they discovered he was alive. And if they had been willing to kill all of these innocent people, who knew what else they had planned?

The plane was pulling up from the dive, just a little bit, but Passenger 36-B's stomach was turning from the forces being exerted on him and the numbing terror of the situation. There was an alarm coming from the cockpit, but he heard no voices in response.

As he put his hands on the door he realized it was probably locked. Wasn't the cockpit door supposed to be secured during the flight? For some reason that sounded right to him. He must have heard the fact somewhere along the way, maybe in his travels, which he couldn't remember anymore.

He tried the latch anyway.

As the door opened, this thought popped into his head again: *82726782B might be faulty.*

He looked through the doorway, found the pilots slumped over in their seats...and he saw why the proximity alarms were sounding.

A runway was rushing toward them at a tremendous rate of speed and although the plane had pulled up a little, it was about to skip across the pavement like a stone on water.

The world shredded around Passenger 36-B in a flash of flames and crunching metal.

———

As the team completed their final search through the wreckage of the commercial airliner and documented the last details for their research, two facts became very clear.

The first fact caused a great deal of joy: the remote controlled crash of the jumbo jet had gone exactly as planned and valuable lessons would be learned.

The second fact wasn't as simple and it might cost someone their job: not only were the electronics in Passenger Simulator 82726782B faulty, as one engineer had suggested, but someone had misplaced the crash test dummy during the prep phase.

The chewed-up remains of the new deluxe Passenger Simulator were nowhere near his assigned seat at the rear of the plane; in fact, he had been found in the burned-out wreckage of the *cockpit* of all places.

Who the hell would have put him there?

the gorman gig

"Jimmy, you've gotta tie the ropes tighter than that."

"I don't know if this is such a good idea."

"Listen, we came here for the money, and we're gonna get the money, you understand me?"

Jimmy put his head down and got back to work. He knew better than to argue with Mike. Jimmy tried his best to secure the woman to the chair, but he had never been good at tying knots and the woman was still squirming and twisting her hands. She probably had a pretty good idea what was happening, even if she didn't know the specifics yet.

Moments earlier Mike had caught her off guard and pushed her down from behind, stuffing a dirty rag into her mouth and forcing a paper grocery bag over her head. She had struggled until she felt the butcher knife against her throat–then she whimpered and did as she was told.

Jimmy yanked on the end of the rope and checked the knot again and found it was as tight as it was going to get. He said: "What do we do now, Mike?"

"Don't use my real name."

"Sorry, Mike. I mean Jake."

"Jesus, Jimmy, you're a real idiot," Mike muttered. "Is your brother watching the street? He's your responsibility, remember?"

"Roger's fine, he's fine. Do you want me to check on him?"

"No, I need you here. This might get messy. Just remember, if your retarded brother screws the pooch, you take the fall."

Mike studied their surroundings. He hadn't expected to see the upstairs of the house. That wasn't part of the plan. The bedroom looked like it belonged on one of the decorating shows his ma was always watching on the premium cable channels. The woman tied to the chair was dressed appropriately for the posh neighborhood, that much was for certain. The bags she had been carrying when she arrived home were now scattered on the floor. Mike checked for anything good, but only found expensive shoes and a new leather handbag.

He watched the woman struggling in the chair, trying to wiggle her way out of the knots, and he felt something stir inside him. He used the knife to cut a few buttons off the woman's fine silk blouse. She flinched. Tears dotted the paper bag covering her head. Mike reached out and squeezed her breast, and she squealed.

"Lady, shut up, okay?" Mike said, startled back into action. "I don't want to have to shut you up. *You* don't want me to shut you up."

BRIAN JAMES FREEMAN

This wasn't how the gig was supposed to go down. Mike and Jimmy were just going to grab the cash and get out of there fast–they hadn't even originally planned to bring Roger along–but the woman had come home earlier than expected.

At least her husband wasn't with her, but considering she had deviated from her routine, who knew when he might arrive. They probably didn't have a lot of time. The husband owned a restaurant and some people said it was a front for something else. For what, Mike wasn't sure, but he knew the guy was loaded and he knew some of the cash was in the house.

"Mike, let's just go. Let's forget the money."

"I know you're scared, Jimmy, but if you use my real name again, I'll cut you and leave you to bleed, you understand me?"

Jimmy shuddered and nodded. This wasn't his style at all. This wasn't what they had planned. This wasn't how the other gigs had gone down.

"Listen to me," Mike said, putting the knife to the woman's throat again. "We just want the money from the basement and we'll let you live, okay? Just tell us where your husband stashed the money and everything will be cool."

The woman mumbled something, but Mike couldn't hear her. He reached under the paper bag and ripped the dirty rag out of her mouth.

"Say it again, real slow, and don't try to scream," he said. "I can kill you before the scream even leaves your throat."

"I don't know what you mean," she whispered, out of breath.

Mike punched the woman in the stomach and she cried a breathless cry. Jimmy jumped backwards, as if *he* had been hit. Mike glanced over and saw his partner trembling and chewing on his fingernails. It wasn't a good sign. He needed Jimmy on his toes for this gig. He certainly couldn't depend on Roger to do anything.

Mike said to the woman: "Tell me where the money is *now*."

"We don't have much in the house," she whispered, sobbing. "I might have a twenty in my purse."

"You lie to me again, I'm gonna hurt you *real* bad."

From the doorway came the familiar stutter: "Mi-Mi-Mikey?"

Mike turned and saw Roger standing there, holding the duffle bag they had brought to carry the money. Mike shook his head and glared at Jimmy, and he didn't have to tell his partner that he was pissed.

Jimmy said: "Roger, you need to watch the front door like we told you. Go back downstairs."

"Bu-bu-but Jimmy? I don-don-don't understand?"

Mike gave Jimmy another look, and this one said, *If you don't handle your retarded brother, I will.*

"Roger, just go downstairs and watch the road, okay? I'll explain everything later. You gotta trust me."

Mike could see the confusion in Roger's eyes, but finally he turned and started back downstairs, his head dipped forward, his eyes locked on his feet. Roger hadn't come along for the first couple of gigs, and those had gone just fine, but plans had changed today and Jimmy had brought his brother along. It couldn't be helped.

"If he comes up here again," Mike said, but Jimmy put his hands up in the air, as if to answer, *I know, I know, you don't have to say anything, don't worry about it.* Mike returned his attention to the woman. "Okay, lady, you've had some time to think about my question, yes?"

"We don't have a lot of money," she whispered.

"Wrong answer." Mike moved to the other side of the chair and put the blade of the knife between her ring finger and her middle finger. She whimpered and started to plead with him to let her go. He shoved the rag back into her mouth to stop her from screaming. He didn't want any neighbors getting suspicious and coming over to see if everything was okay. Things were definitely not okay.

Mike pressed on the knife, gently splitting the flesh between the woman's fingers. She screamed but the sound was muffled. Blood sprayed onto the white carpet.

"Mike, no," Jimmy said as he turned away, but he never finished the statement. He fainted and hit the floor like a sack of potatoes.

"Christ, what a bunch of losers I'm working with," Mike muttered. He stared at the blood dripping between the fingers of the woman's tightly held fist. The puddle was soaking into the carpet. He said: "Listen lady, I don't want to hurt you more than I have to, you understand? Just tell us what we want to know."

"Mi-Mi-Mikey?"

Mike's head snapped up at the sound of the stutter and he was already starting to tell Roger to go back down the fucking stairs when he realized his unwanted partner-in-crime wasn't alone. A man in a black suit stood in the doorway beside Roger. A big man. Taller and heavier than Mike remembered.

"What are you doing, you son of a bitch?" the man asked. The woman reacted strongly to the sound of her husband's voice, struggling against the chair and calling his name in a muffled cry. Mike quickly placed the bloody knife against her throat. She became still again.

"Hey man," Mike said. "Put your hands in the air. We just want the money in your basement and we'll let her live." He glanced over at Jimmy, who was lying next to the bed, disoriented from his fall. "Jimmy, get off the fuckin' floor."

"Oh crap," Jimmy whispered, blinking his eyes and trying to stand. He saw Roger. He saw the husband. "Oh shit!"

"Listen, I don't know what you mean," the husband said, holding his hands up. "What money?"

"I heard you talking about it so don't lie to me again," Mike said. "You lie and your wife gets a new hole to breathe through. I heard you say you put twenty grand into your basement and I want it."

"No, you misunderstood. I meant renovations. I finished the basement into a rec room and that's what it cost me. Twenty grand. There's no cash in the house."

"Mike, let's just get out of here," Jimmy said. "Mister, you'll let us go if we don't hurt your wife, right?"

Mike turned to tell Jimmy to shut the fuck up, but the moment his attention shifted, the husband leapt across the room and knocked him down to the floor, moving faster than Mike ever imagined possible. The knife flew from his hand and the man quickly recovered it.

The man braced his knee on Mike's chest, easily holding him on the floor. The woman cried in the darkness under the brown bag.

"Sit over there, in the corner," the man said, pointing the bloody knife at Jimmy and Roger. They complied without hesitation. This wasn't right. This wasn't how the gig was supposed to go down, and they had no idea what to do without

Mike telling them. Roger started to cry. The front of his pants turned dark when he wet himself.

The man pulled the paper bag off his wife's head and he removed the rag from her mouth. He cut the rope with one precise movement of the knife, freeing her hands. She jumped to her feet and backed away from her attackers.

"You okay, hon?" the man asked.

"I'll live," his wife replied, clutching her hands together tightly, massaging her bloody fingers. "Thank God you came home when you did."

The man pushing down on Mike's chest was heavy and strong, and Mike had to battle just to keep breathing. He saw the terror growing on the faces of his friends and he realized he was probably going to see the inside of a police car for the first time in his life.

"You know the cops ain't gonna do anything to us!" Mike said, coughing out the words as the pressure inside his lungs grew worse. He was terrified, but he didn't want to show his fear. "They ain't gonna throw the book at a bunch of middle school kids!"

"Maybe not," the man said as he pressed his knee down harder. "But I don't think we need to get the law involved. You ever see those kids on the *Missing* posters?"

the punishment room

michael wasn't sure how long he had been chained naked to the floor of the Big Man's Punishment Room, but he did know the Big Man would be coming back soon. Then the bleeding and the screaming and the torture would start again.

The coldness of the Punishment Room had long ago seeped through Michael's skin and taken hold of his bones. The smooth concrete floor and the metal drain near his feet were stained with dried blood. He was a young man, but his back ached like he was a hundred years old thanks to he strain of sitting in the same position for days on end. Directly across from Michael was a wide mirror that relentlessly showed his reflection. He couldn't help but stare into it, watching himself deteriorate.

There were no windows in the Punishment Room, of course, just that damned mirror, so Michael had lost track of time. The hours between the Big Man's visits were horrible and the nights were full of their own terrors, but now the nightmares weren't nearly as bad as what happened when Michael was awake. In fact, the nightmares were almost comforting in their own bizarre way. At least in his dreams, he was in control. He didn't have to do the terrible things the Big Man demanded or face the consequences for non-compliance.

Assuming Michael managed to escape this hellhole with his sanity and his life–and those odds were looking worse and worse with each passing visit of the Big Man–he wasn't sure if he'd be able to go on living with the knowledge of what he had done to survive. Then again, that was a dilemma he wouldn't mind being forced to deal with, given the finality of the alternative.

When the Big Man entered the Punishment Room like clockwork and made his unspoken demands, Michael would do what he had to do to keep on living for another day, his eyes never leaving his own reflection in the mirror.

The Big Man always gave Michael the same two options, and Michael hated the cold eyes staring back at him in the mirror as he made his choice. He never stopped staring at himself, judging himself for what he had done, contemplating how he had ended up here in the first place.

Michael knew he might eventually escape from this endless hell–there was always a slim chance, he was certain of that–but there was no escaping his own tired, bloodshot eyes.

Some days he gazed at his reflection for so long he felt like he was watching someone else, a spooky feeling under the best of conditions.

The growing darkness in his eyes scared him, but what else could he do?

Michael sat and waited and watched the mirror. He barely recognized the man in the reflection, sitting upright against a bloodstained cinderblock wall. His hands were chained to heavy anchors in the floor, but he had enough range of movement to do what the Big Man demanded if he didn't want to suffer more than necessary. If he didn't want to choose his other option.

Day after day after day passed. The nightmares grew worse and the Big Man's terrible choices became more maddening.

Michael's body and mind were exhausted. His eyes burned from the horror of the things he had seen and done. Soon there was movement in the mirror when he was all alone. Darkness shifting and jumping in the corners. His own eyes, big and red and tired, peering back at him, searching for some escape from the terror. The eyes in the mirror moved while his own eyes remained still.

And as always, after another string of endless hours spent staring at himself, watching those strange eyes he didn't recognize, Michael heard the footsteps echoing down the stairs. The door hidden in the corner of the room opened.

Michael's heart raced and he closed his eyes for the first time in hours. He didn't want to know what the next punishment would be–and he definitely didn't want to see who the Big Man might have brought with him today.

Yet keeping his eyes closed meant nothing when he heard the small voice whisper: "Mikey?"

Michael's eyes flew open and he stared in horror. His little sister stood next to the Big Man, who was dressed all in black with the mask protecting his face. Alicia wore her best Sunday dress and she had obviously been crying.

"No, no, no," Michael said, his voice a low growl like some kind of trapped animal.

The Big Man towered above Alicia and he led her by the hand. His gloved hand was huge, engulfing her small fingers, but his grip wasn't tight and Alicia didn't struggle the way Michael had when he first awoke in this terrible place. Her eyes were big, yet she showed no fear.

In her left hand, Alicia held a pair of pliers.

"Oh Alicia, no," Michael whispered. He tried to believe she was a hallucination–maybe he had finally lost his mind for good, maybe this was just another nightmare–but he had known the truth the instant he heard her voice.

The Big Man released Alicia's hand and she crossed the room and sat down on the floor in front of her big brother.

"I'm sorry," she said, her eyes locked on his face.

Michael began to cry. So did she.

The Big Man watched the events unfold with his usual detached silence. This was *his* room–he controlled what happened and when, yet he said nothing.

"I am, too," Michael replied, staring at the grimy metal drain in the concrete floor. He couldn't even look his little sister in the eyes as he considered his options one more time.

He could finally take his own life and end the pain for good–which would also allow his little sister to go free without suffering through the horror of what was to come–or he could accept what the Big Man silently demanded.

These were the same two options Michael was presented every evening–just with a different person waiting in front of him, holding a different tool or weapon–and as Michael grew more tired, as the eyes in the mirror became darker and darker, the two options seemed more and more similar.

Michael looked at Alicia. She nodded and tried to hand him the pliers.

She was closer to him than anyone in the world, but deep down Michael knew he wanted to live for another day.

Another hellish, terrible day.

Another day of hoping to escape.

Another day of praying to live to regret what he had done.

Just one more day.

Michael watched in the mirror as the stranger he didn't recognize took the pliers and did what needed to be done.

———————

Later, after the Big Man had disposed of yet another body, the pool of Alicia's blood continued to drip down the metal drain in the middle of the floor while Michael stared at the stranger's eyes in the mirror.

He didn't blink for the longest time, but his mouth moved silently.

After a few minutes of this unspoken conversation with his reflection, Michael grinned and pulled his left hand close to his mouth, the chains growing taut between him and the heavy anchor in the floor.

He chewed on his wrist.

The blood came soon after.

———————

"Oh my God! I can't stand to watch this anymore!"

Like always, the gray haired lady had been given the best seat in the house: a stiff, plastic chair directly on the other side of the large two-way mirror facing the prisoner.

The viewing room was cold and sterile, and the witnesses for the State murmured at the latest development. Michael Cooper, prisoner 82726782B, really *was* chewing at his wrist.

"That's acceptable, Mrs. Lawson," the Government Official said from his leather chair in the control booth. "Mr. Cooper's punishment ends as soon as you tell us he's been rehabilitated and your family is satisfied that society has been repaid for his crimes. Is this what you're saying?"

The little old woman rubbed her face with her brittle fingers and contemplated what had happened since the prisoner ran out of appeals, what had been done on the other side of the mirror, the horrors she had witnessed.

She whispered: "I just never imagined it would be so…gruesome. The way he keeps staring at me…"

"You can set him free whenever you'd like. That is how the system works, after all."

The old woman sat behind the mirror, watching the boy who had killed her granddaughter. She watched him and her heart dropped into her stomach and she heard her granddaughter's sweet laughter at a Thanksgiving dinner long lost to the past.

The old woman flinched as the boy chewed at his bloody arm, and she asked herself again and again how much more she could really stand to see, to hear, before she'd go mad. How much more punishment did this boy deserve until everything had been made right? And how much more could *she* take?

Then she remembered that cold day when she heard the piercing scream outside and she rushed out to find her granddaughter's bloody and broken body in the middle of the street in front of the house.

The little girl never had a chance against that car.

The old woman remembered all of this for the millionth time and then she said: "I think I can stand the sight for another day. Just one more day."

And then she watched the prisoner consume his own flesh while the witnesses for the State whispered their words of reassurance.

the silent attic

my name is Amy Walker and my mother died three years ago on a sweltering August day during the worst heat wave in decades.

Any time spent in the direct sunlight that week risked a quick burn. Walking outside was like being wrapped in a wool blanket.

I was fifteen.

My little brother was just three.

My father was forty going on forever.

He worked two shifts at the factory to keep the bills paid and we rarely saw him. He worked so hard because he loved us, but also, I believe, because the work allowed him to pretend his wife wasn't dying.

The cancer started in my mother's breast and spread quickly, undetected. She was never the same person after the doctor appointment when she received the bad news.

Sometimes I think she actually died that day.

The rest of the time, the time spent in the upstairs bedroom of our little Cape Cod style house, the time spent wasting away, didn't count for anything.

My mother had been so full of life, so energetic before the cancer. She deftly juggled kids and work and mortgage payments and car insurance and everything else, and she did so with a smile and an easy laugh.

After that visit to the doctor, she was a shell of a broken woman.

Within days she looked weak and pale and near death, as if she had been holding back the grim reaper without ever knowing it, but now she had given up the fight.

I spent a lot of time by my mother's side that summer, but I also had to watch Daniel, and he was a handful.

Caring for your three-year-old brother when you're a teenager, when you spent the first twelve years of your life as an only child, is strange, to say the least, but you learn to play the cards you're dealt, as one of my dad's poker buddies from BC (before cancer) used to say.

As my mother got sicker, I took over her responsibilities the best I could.

I'd clean the house and do the laundry and make sure dinner was ready when my father arrived home at nine o'clock each night.

He'd drag himself in through the front door, his blue overalls black with grease, his face and hands caked with smears of oil, his legs moving like pillars of granite.

He'd wash his hands for half an hour to get the grit out from under his nails and then we'd eat in silence at the little table in the kitchen. Daniel was already in bed.

I'd wash the dishes while Dad showered and I'd pack his lunch for the next day, just like my mother used to pack my lunch when I was a kid, and then Dad would go upstairs and spend the rest of the night holding my mother while she slept.

I'll never forget how the attic bedroom smelled of a long, painful illness that summer.

I loved my mother, but I hated that smell.

The attic was small and cozy, with a box fan in one of the windows blowing hot, humid air across the room. There were white, lacy curtains in the other window, which was usually left open for ventilation.

The queen-sized bed was against the far wall, with two matching nightstands and a chair from the kitchen.

I'd sit on that chair and hold my mom's hand and she'd sleep and sometimes she'd want to talk but speaking was difficult for her in those last weeks.

I'd sit there and try not to see how small my mother was, how the cancer had hollowed her out.

Every day she lay under the covers, under the heavy Amish blanket my father had bought her for Christmas the year before.

The house was sweltering, but she was always so cold.

On the day she died, my mother could barely speak, but she whispered she was thirsty and needed a drink of water.

I dutifully went downstairs to the kitchen, got a clean glass, and filled it halfway.

I thought about checking on my brother.

He was napping in his room at the end of the hallway and the visit would give me a little more time away from that awful attic.

From the smell of impending death.

But I couldn't move. My legs wouldn't let me take a step.

I stood in the kitchen, closed my eyes, and found myself sinking into the memory of a trip to Black Rock Lake on a beautiful spring day.

The sky was blue and cloudless, the breeze was light and pleasant. Birds chirped in the trees, fish practically leapt from the sparkling lake water, and the sandy beach by the campground was golden and perfect in every way.

That was the last and happiest trip my family took before the cancer, and I wished with all of my might that I could travel back in time to that day and grab myself and yell: "Don't let go of this! Stay here, forever! Life will never be better than this day!"

The memory was so real and so strong that I was disappointed when I opened my eyes and found myself standing in the stifling, humid kitchen.

Half an hour had passed.

The movement of my legs as I climbed the steps to the attic bedroom felt wrong, like I was trapped in slow motion.

Something inside me stirred, trembled.

The fan in the window had turned off again, but that wasn't unusual. The motor had been dying for years now and often overheated.

My legs shook and when I pushed the door to the attic bedroom open far enough to see the bed, I stopped.

I looked into the room, which was lit by the sunlight sneaking in around the curtains.

Dirty, blinding light.

My mom's eyes were open, glassy and staring at the ceiling, but she wasn't breathing.

I had known this was coming but I wasn't ready.

I hadn't truly believed the end was near or that the end was even really going to come.

Maybe I was waiting on a miracle. Or maybe I was just a dumb kid.

I made my way to the bed, although I don't remember taking a step, and with a trembling hand I closed my mother's eyes.

Her papery skin was cold to the touch and yet sweat still beaded across her brow.

I sat on the edge of the bed, soaking in the sweltering heat, and I listened to the silence.

I had never heard the house so quiet.

I sat and I sipped from the glass of water, both sad and happy and devastated and relieved.

My mother had been in so much pain.

I sipped the water until the glass slipped out of my hand, shattering on the hardwood floor.

Then I cried.

Downstairs I heard Daniel begin to cry, too. The noise had scared him.

I stood, careful not to step on the broken glass, and I made my way down to my brother's bedroom.

I held Daniel and I told him about Mom and I comforted him as he cried.

I called my father and he rushed home.

A very nice man from the funeral home picked up my mother less than an hour later, and the funeral came and went the following afternoon, and we all cried and the days passed in a blur.

And then, before I knew it, I was home alone watching my brother while my father returned to work.

I'd watch Daniel and I'd sit on the couch and I'd fight the urge to go upstairs to check on Mom.

While Daniel napped, I would lie on the couch and close my eyes.

I would no longer be in the living room.

Instead I'd be with my mother on her last day of life.

Maybe that's why I've had these bad dreams since my mother died, four or five times a week for the last three years.

In the nightmares I'm fifteen again, filling a glass of water half-full in the kitchen. The glass is for my mother, and I have to go and find her dead body.

I know this and I can't stop myself.

One moment I'm in the kitchen, the next I'll be standing at the top of the stairs holding the glass of water.

I push on the door.

My mother is in the bed, lying under dusty covers that haven't been changed in three years, her body frail and thin.

The light coming in through the windows is dirty and the room is so hot the air shimmers like the distant horizon of a desert.

My mother's face has been covered with the blanket.

She has died again and yet again, I wasn't here.

"Mother needs her water," I whisper, my voice cracking like I'm a small child.

"Yes, I do," comes the raspy reply.

My mother growls as she sits up, the sheet wrapping around her like a burial shroud, the blanket sliding off her face.

She asks: "Why did you leave me up here to die? Why didn't you help me?"

The window flies open and a cold winter wind, the antithesis of the heat that enveloped me all summer long, gusts through the space, blowing the sheets off my mother's corpse.

I cry out at the sight.

My mother has been waiting a long time for me to return.

Her ribs poke through her gaunt belly and her breasts are deflated, saggy.

Her face is tight and dry like a mummy. Her eyes are cold and fogged.

A single, bloody tear trickles across her crooked nose.

She opens her mouth.

She points one bony finger at me and says: "If only you had brought the water faster, I wouldn't be dead!"

"No, no, that's not true!" I whimper, the terror inside me was as real as anything I've ever felt.

Usually that fear is enough to wake me before my mom gets out of the bed and stumbles across the room, but not always.

Every now and then she'll get her skeleton-like arms around me for a hug.

Often I wake up screaming.

I don't find sleep easily after the nightmares.

Sometimes I'm awake the rest of the night.

Sometimes I'm so thirsty.

I hate that dream.

I think of the silent attic and I miss my mother.

My family is hollow without her.

a dreamlike state

When Danny Walker was a child, when he was six years old and Christmas came and went and he finally understood that his sister was never coming home again, nightmares consumed his nights–even the nights when he couldn't sleep at all.

He would lie in bed with the covers pulled up to his chin, his overactive imagination wildly analyzing the moving shadows created by the light in the hallway outside his room. His closet door would creak open and glowing eyes would stare at him from behind his shirts and pants. Broken fingernails would tap on the hardwood floor under his bed and he was certain he could hear something breathing down there.

Finally, when Danny thought he could endure no more, his dead sister's voice spoke to him from the darkness.

Amy whispered the last words she ever said to him before her death and the sound of her voice forced the monsters away and brought Danny enough comfort to sleep through the rest of the night.

———————

Today Daniel Walker's cold hands tremble on the steering wheel as he navigates the cracked and broken road to the small mining town he called home for the first eighteen years of his life, a haunted placed called Black Hills that he hasn't seen since the day of his high school graduation.

dreamlike states

Daniel drives in silence. The only sounds are the slick whisper of wet pavement under the car's tires, the growl of the engine, and the wind howling across the valley like a wounded animal. He hears that same angry cry in the night whenever he closes his eyes, when he struggles for the sleep that won't come.

His chronic insomnia began the night his sister told him she was never coming home, but the lack of sleep hasn't left him for dead like he once thought it would. He's simply another one of the walking-wounded drifting through a shell of a life full of moving shadows and dead-end streets.

Amy died when Daniel was six years old and she was eighteen–two months after her boyfriend vanished into the night, never to be seen again, and all of the terrible rumors started–and Daniel has never forgotten how his big sister brought a chair into his bedroom while their father worked a double-shift at the factory, how she sat and explained what she had to do.

And even though Daniel had no intention of ever seeing his father again once he was able to make his own cobbled-together life in the city, today he finds himself parked in front of his childhood home.

The wood siding needs a good coat of paint and two of the shutters are hanging crooked. The lawn is white with snow and brown with dead grass. The overgrown shrubs under the windows bend wildly from the weight of the ice that has fallen from the overflowing gutters. The driveway has not been shoveled since the last storm.

The sun is setting and Daniel knows his father is sleeping inside the house, but Frank Walker won't be in the upstairs bedroom he shared with his wife until the cancer came for her. In his final days, he's confined to one of the two bedrooms on the first floor. He can no longer handle the stairs.

His father isn't old enough to be dying, at least in Daniel's mind, but the knot in his gut tells him otherwise. There will soon be another ghost to keep him awake at night.

Daniel quietly enters the house. The rooms are dark and night is claiming the world, but the interior of the home is exactly as he remembers it: the wood floors are dull and scuffed, the stairs up to the master bedroom are dusty.

In the hallway to the first floor bedrooms are four framed photographs, none of them recent.

One is Anne, Daniel's mother, the year before the cancer took her. Next is Amy on the day of her confirmation at church, standing in a row with all of the other bored seventh graders. Third is Daniel as a baby in his mother's arms.

The last photo is a candid shot of Amy with Charlie McBride, the shy and friendly teenager who moved to town six months before Amy died, the only boy Daniel's sister ever truly loved. This photo was taken out at Black Rock Lake by one of their friends, probably Susan.

Daniel's childhood bedroom is at the end of the hallway. He can hear an oxygen machine hissing and sighing in that room. He carefully navigates the hallway's squeaky floorboards and, after pausing for a moment, he reluctantly pushes the door open.

His father is lying in the small bed and he looks fifty years older than the last time Daniel saw him. His face is wrinkled, his hair is gray, his arms are bone skinny. He blinks his eyes open when the light from the hallway creeps across the bed. His mouth opens. A drip of spit bridges the open gap between his yellowed and missing teeth.

"Danny?"

"Yeah, Pop, it's me."

"Please open the blinds."

Daniel obediently pulls the curtains back, letting in the last rays of colorless winter sunlight.

"Didn't anyone ever teach you how to knock?"

"Sorry, Pop," Daniel says, like a child scolded. He sits on the wooden chair by the side of the bed.

"Danny, you blame me for your sister's death, don't you?"

No small talk. Not today.

Daniel whispers, "That's the past."

He's saying something he doesn't believe, but he has become very good at spinning lies–to himself and to others. His entire life is a tapestry of lies: he lives in the city because he wants to live there; he doesn't sleep at night because he doesn't really need to sleep; the haggard lines tattooed on his face from the nightmares are invisible to others.

For Daniel the lies create an acceptable way to live. He lies because he has to lie. To tell the truth would be suicide.

"You feeling okay, Pop?"

"Mind's foggy. Weak."

"You want me to get you some water?"

"No, we should talk. Did you have a good drive?"

"It was fine. Everything seems the same."

"Things have changed, boy, but they change slowly." Frank pauses, then adds: "I miss your sister."

"I miss her, too."

"Her and your mother and you. But you're the only one who has ever come back to me."

"You're looking good, Pop," Daniel says, desperate to change the subject. He's sitting on the edge of the wooden chair like he might need to bolt from the room in a heartbeat. His father smiles weakly.

"Liar, liar," Frank whispers. Then, a moment later, he demands: "Why are you so late getting home? It's past your curfew. You weren't sneaking out with that Natalie girl again, were you?"

Frank Walker is no longer in the present. He isn't living in the same year as the rest of the world. He has slipped back in time and he's asking about a girl Daniel dated in high school, a girl Daniel hasn't spoken with in six years.

"No, Pop, I wasn't. It's not past my curfew yet," Daniel says, taking hold of his father's hands.

"It isn't?"

"No, Pop, it's not."

"It's dark in here," the old man who shouldn't be so old whispers. He opens his mouth to say something else, but no words come and his eyes close and quickly he's asleep, his mouth gaping open like a door with broken hinges, dribble forming at the corners of his lips.

Daniel sits and watches his father take shallow breaths. This is the same man who once struck him in a drunken fit after Amy died and yet it's not the same man at all. The hollow human in front of Daniel looks more like the remorseful father who pleaded with his son to forgive him for the bruises the next day. This is a man who lost his wife to cancer and then his daughter to suicide and then finally his son to…to what? A desperate attempt to escape the past?

Daniel has never forgotten the conflicting stories he heard after Amy died: the speculation, the gossip, the official reports from the police, the local newspaper's editorials. None of the stories completely matched each other and none of them told the complete truth.

A cold whisper passes through the back of Daniel's mind, leaving as quietly as it came and barely registering: *Sometimes after I fall, I bleed.*

The words trigger a memory he hasn't thought about in nearly two decades and he shudders as the images resurface, feeling more like a movie than anything real.

———

When Danny Walker was six years old, in the days and weeks and months after his sister died, the nightmares were as bad as the monsters he imagined in the darkness of his bedroom. Sometimes they were worse.

Sleep became harder and harder to find until he could only huddle in his bed, wide-awake and terrified, listening to his father sobbing in the bedroom above. He would count the minutes as they passed and he would wait for the darkness to close in around him.

Then one night, as he hid under the covers with his eyes held tightly closed, Danny had an idea, one that seemed too brilliant to be his own.

Amy had whispered this idea into his ear, he was sure of it.

Danny knew what people would say if he told them his dead sister was speaking to him, but he believed in his heart she had given him this plan, and to his six-year-old mind it was simple enough to work: he would create an imaginary world to escape into as darkness descended upon the real world.

Danny's heart raced as he closed his eyes and attempted to conjure up the happiest place he could imagine.

There was simple darkness behind his eyelids at first, but then images formed, blurry and indecipherable.

He concentrated harder and memories streamed through the darkness: his mother and Amy at a family picnic; Miss Wilson, his kindergarten teacher, at the front of the classroom passing out modeling clay; Mr. Whiskers, the neighbor's overweight cat, trying to stalk a bird through the lawn; a lion in a cage at the Pittsburgh Zoo with funny-looking fur.

Finally Danny's mind landed on the memory of a trip to Black Rock Lake on a beautiful spring day, and he grabbed onto this image with all his might.

The sky was blue and cloudless.

The breeze was light and pleasant.

Birds chirped in the trees.

Fish practically leapt from the clear, crisp water.

The sandy beach by the campground was golden and perfect in every way.

The woods hummed and everything seemed to glow with the energy of the living things contained within.

And best of all, Amy was there, holding his hand like they had found each other through the darkness.

A large wooden sign, which in the real world appeared at the entrance to the park's gravel parking lot, floated in the water near the beach.

In the real world this sign said: WELCOME TO BLACK ROCK LAKE.

In Daniel's newly created imaginary world the sign said: WELCOME TO THE DARK COUNTRY.

Although the name was sinister, the land was not, and for a while Danny *was* able to sleep soundly through the night if he closed his eyes and imagined himself in the Dark Country.

He would swim in the clear water and lie under the hot sun and play with as many friends as his imagination could create, always with Amy by his side, smiling and very much alive.

But one night Danny closed his eyes and took himself to the Dark Country and Amy didn't appear like she usually did–and he couldn't find her no matter how hard he tried.

Soon, as night after night came and went without any sign of Amy, the sun in the imaginary land drifted down the sky, shifting the world from a mid-afternoon in early summer to the dim nothingness of a cold January evening. The water grew dark and murky, and his imaginary friends transformed into monsters of the night.

Danny never saw Amy again and the rest of the sunny barriers protecting him in the Dark Country crumbled–and not long after, his imaginary world turned poisonous. He would never be able to return.

Years would pass and he'd forget the Dark Country, but the nightmares wouldn't end and peaceful sleep never returned, not even after he fled the town where his personal demons roamed like gods.

———

Daniel raises his hand to wipe the hot tears from his face. He pushes the thoughts away and he quietly leaves his father's side, closing the bedroom door and turning off the hallway light. He's exhausted and he has no desire to think about the Dark Country, not ever again.

Instead he wants to clear his head and understand why he really came home. Why he *really* made this trip today. Was it simply because of his father's deteriorating health? Or was there another reason?

A small voice in the back of Daniel's mind asks if he has finally come to confront the truth about what happened to his sister, but he ignores the question. He knew Amy as well as you can know your sister when she is twelve years your elder and she dies young, which isn't very well at all, at least in his experience.

She seemed as old as any adult to him. Twelve years between siblings is an almost impassable canyon as far as he is concerned. His sister might as well have been a total stranger living in his home...and yet he loved her fiercely and blamed himself completely once he understood she was never coming back.

After Amy's death, Daniel carried a lot of weight on his shoulders, a lot of guilt. He carried a town's worth of guilt for twelve years, then he graduated high school–something his sister never did–and he fled to the city where he's been ever since, where he has spent countless nights imagining what his sister's life might have been like if things had gone differently, imagining how different *his* life could have been.

Daniel enters Amy's bedroom, pushing the door open with a certain reverence. The room became a monument, a shrine, following his sister's death. Nothing has been altered. Everything is the same. The bed. The writing desk. The books on the bookcases. The pink paint on the walls, faded by time. The lacy curtains. The dolls on the shelf, forgotten by his sister in the years leading up to her death.

There is a surprising amount of dust and cobwebs in the room, though, and Daniel realizes his father has been sick for longer than he was told.

He closes the door and returns to the dark living room, stopping at the stairs to the master bedroom, the only room on the second floor of the house.

There's a door at the top of the steps and a rickety handrail along the wall. He almost never saw the inside of the room when he was a child, but now he stares at the door.

Since his father is sleeping in Daniel's room, and Daniel would never dare sleep in his sister's room, he has no choice of where to go if he wants to lie in the dark for a while and pretend he might be able to rest tonight.

He forces himself to climb the stairs, open the door, and make his way to the bed by the light of the new moon coming in the round window at the end of the narrow space. The wind shrieks past the house and this is the sound he remembers from the endless nights of his haunted youth. To him the wind sounds like a nightmare screaming.

Daniel crawls under the stiff Amish quilt and he closes his eyes, but he does not sleep. Sleep would only bring dreams of Amy and her body sinking into the icy cold water of Black Rock Lake the day before Christmas–and the rest of the nightmares would grow worse from there.

Yet after a while something like a dream does begin, but he doesn't believe he's sleeping, he can't be sleeping.

If this is a dream, it's one he has never experienced before; this would be his first new dream in more than eighteen years.

Daniel is a child again and he's sitting in the woods and he's terrified. He's cold and alarmed and he's blind and something is growing inside of him, eating him alive, eating him so fast he can hear the teeth chewing.

Deep in his core Daniel understands he has returned to the Dark Country–some forbidden corner of his imaginary world he never traveled through as a child. He has come home and the Dark County was here waiting for him all along.

Even though he's blind, he can hear a wild beast stalking through the woods. Twigs snap. Branches break. There's movement everywhere. The air is cold and his flesh trembles. The woods are closing in, swallowing him. The trees loom above him, the branches reaching to hold him in place for the monster's gaping jaws.

He wants to scream, but he can't–his mouth is sewn shut.

A shadow envelopes Daniel's face and he realizes he's *not* blind–his eyes are merely closed.

He forces his eyes open and again he wants to scream.

Charlie McBride, the shy and friendly teenager who moved to town and started dating Amy Walker and then vanished into the night without a trace, stands there as a teenager who has never aged…but he's no longer friendly or shy.

Charlie towers over Daniel, large and monstrous. His skull is smashed and his eye sockets are broken and bleeding.

This is not a young man who disappeared because he chose not to be found.

This is not someone who disappeared of his own free will.

Deep down Daniel has always known this truth. It's what the nightmares have been screaming at him for years, but he hasn't wanted to believe them. How could he believe them?

This monster version of Charlie reaches for Daniel, touching his face with hands made of glassy ice.

"Sometimes after I fall," Charlie whispers as blood trickles from between his lips, "I bleed." His hands squeeze Daniel's face, harder and harder. "I bleed, Amy," Charlie says. "*I bleed.*"

And then Daniel opens his eyes in the real world, awakening from the dreamlike state that isn't close enough to sleep to be worth the terror growing inside of him. He's soaked in sweat, his arms are folded across his chest and he's squeezing so hard he fears his bones might break.

Daniel lets go and rolls to his side, toward the nightstand. He glances at the ancient alarm clock's glowing green face. Only five minutes have passed since he came upstairs.

He remains in the dark, his breathing heavy, his heart pounding. He knows the demons of the past aren't real, but their sharp teeth bite into him like razors. They *are* part of his life, just like the haggard worry lines on his face.

Daniel breathes out deeply. He can still hear Charlie McBride whisper: *Sometimes after I fall, I bleed.*

He recalls the rumors and attacks whispered around town when he was a child, the whispering that drove him away to the city as soon as he was old enough, the whispers that gave birth to the nightmares that haunt him.

Daniel stares at the moonlit ceiling, his breathing slowly coming under his control again, and he listens for his father to stir downstairs. The house is silent and this bedroom feels like a tomb.

Daniel watches the shadows dance around the ceiling and he knows the demons of his past will have much more to tell him before the morning light creeps across the winter wasteland that is his childhood home…but as he trembles in the darkened bedroom he begins to feel something like hope, an emotion so foreign it terrifies him.

With the birth of this new nightmare, he senses something is different now, although he can't quite put his finger on what that difference might be.

Maybe there are answers in these dreams, answers that will set him free.

Maybe.

Maybe coming home will finally set him free of the past.

Maybe.

Daniel closes his eyes and his last thought as he falls asleep is simple:

Sometimes after I fall, I bleed.

CHADBOURNE